Clint Faraday
book thirty eight
Dead Reckoning

Clint and family are enjoying their last two weeks this trip at their place in Quebrada Tula. Basilio, from Cusapín, is visiting. They are sitting on the porch at sunset, which is spectacular. Basilio says there is going to be trouble. It is in the signs. It will involve people on the comarca, but will not be from the comarca.

Clint remembers other times when Basilio made predictions based on a special sunset. He figured he could depend on hearing about exactly that.

Then, the body.

Contents

About the author

CD Moulton has traveled extensively over much of the world both in the music business, where he was a rock guitarist, songwriter and arranger and in an import/export business. He has been everything from a bar owner to auto salvage (junkyard) manager, longshoreman to high steel worker, orchid grower to landscaper, tropical fish farmer to commercial fisherman. He started writing books in 1983 and has published more than 350 books as of January 1, 2023. His most popular books to date are about research with orchids, though much of his science fiction and fantasy work has proven popular. He wrote the CD Grimes, PI series, and the Det. Nick Storie series, Clint Faraday series, and many other works.

He now resides in Gualaca, Chiriqui, Panamá, where he writes books, plays music with friends, does research with orchids and medicinal plants. He has lately become involved in fighting for the rights of the indigenous people, who are among his closest friends, and in fighting the extreme corruption in the courts and police in Panamá.

He offers the free e-book, *Fading Paradise*, that explains what he has been through because of the corruption.

CD is the discoverer of the Chadam Protocol for curing cancer.

Facebook page Ambrosia peruviana for cancer.

Dead Reckoning

Sunrise Spectacular

Clint Faraday, retired PI, originally from Florida, now living in Panamá, handed Basilio, chief of the Ngobe Bugle comarca in Cusapín, a cup of coffee and sat in silence to watch the amazing display of pinks and salmons and golds play across the early dawning sky. Sunrises could be spectacular here, and often were.

Clint enjoyed the great honor of having been declared Ngobe by the council. He was the second white person ever to be so honored. His wife was Ngobe, and his young son was being raised in the Ngobe traditions. It was a very different life than Clint had known before coming here.

"The light is beautiful on the water and coming onto the beach," Balilio commented. "There is a face. It seems to be wanting to tell me something this morning. A reckoning. I must study this a moment."

Clint knew how the atmospheric conditions could produce what were termed "omens" by the people who understood them. Basilio had several times before made predictions that had proven eerily accurate.

Nito, Clint's two year old son, came out to hand Basilio a plate of patacones to go with the superb coffee. Basilio loved the fried banana patties the way Tyna, Clint's beautiful wife, cooked them. Nito returned a moment later with a plate of hojaldres for Clint and climbed into his lap to have one himself. Tyna brought a plate of fish-cakes for them all. She brought a cinnamon pancake for herself. Clint taught her how to make them. She preferred the cinnamon pancakes, while Basilio preferred the patacones. Clint preferred hojaldres. Nito liked all of it (as did they all), but hojaldres were special.

"Hmm. The signs are very good for most, but there is something ... there is great danger for someone. Death is possible ... I cannot tell who. It is not a person here," Basilio said seriously. "I do not like when the signs are ambiguous. It too often means they are not for here except ... they affect things here.

"Well, we can't do anything about it. There is no reason for special preparations among us.

"Nito, I saw you with the new gringos yesterday afternoon. You were with their son. He's older than you in body, but is a baby in mind. You did not stay?"

"I do not understand him. My Dad says he acts

like that because he's from another culture."

Two years old. The Indio children can shock you with what seems their maturity at times.

"What happened?" Tyna asked.

"I don't know. He wanted some helado and his mother said he couldn't have it so close to dinner. He started yelling and crying and she bought him one. He wanted some galletas to go with it and she just acted like she didn't know what to do. He started yelling again and she bought him some.

"I don't think I like him. I don't think I can like his mother. He's lazy and ... I don't know. She is the mother. Why doesn't she act like a mother? She is the boss. If she says 'No!' it is 'No!' but she won't do it. Doesn't she care how she will make him a ladrone and chulo?"

"She doesn't know how to raise children," Tyna said.

"He has no place," Basilio said, simply. Tyna and Clint nodded. Nito thought a moment very seriously, then slowly nodded. "I think that was why. It looked like that to me. I am here because my mother and father want me to be here. I have my things to do. I am here because I am Ngobe. This is my place. He is only ... here."

Clint was often amazed at how wise a two year old could sound, but that was simply the Indio philosophy. At two years of age Nito had his responsibilities to the family, first, and to the Ngobe Bugle, as a whole, second. He was almost constantly in physical contact with one or the other of his parents and siblings (when he had any). He shared in their lives. He was here with adults so was part of the conversation. No one tried to get him to "Go play!" or anything. Clint felt that was the entire basis of the philosophy of raising children. His son never doubted for one second that he was loved and wanted. *He had a place.*

"I never had a reason to exist before I came here," he said, aloud. The others didn't reply. It wasn't necessary.

"I do!" Nito said. He hugged Clint tightly, then said he would get the eggs and see that the garden didn't have a lot of bugs this morning. He went down the steps and to the lush vegetable garden behind the house. Tyna came to sit on the lap Nito had vacated.

"The light is going into day," Basilio said. "The signs for all here were good, but for someone, bad. As always is with you Clint will become involved in some manner, but he can find what is behind it.

"That isn't in the signs. It's just how things are when Clint Faraday is in the same country!"

They joked and laughed awhile until Basilio said

he would have to get back home to his own family. He said he would have to be careful or his children (18, 20 and 21 years old) would turn out to be gringos in Ngobe skin. They were getting lazy just because he was chief. Here it was near to six o'clock and they were probably just now getting out of bed!

That was a joke, of course. It was based on the Latinos and gringos who didn't get out of bed until eight o'clock or later to be at work at nine. The Indios worked from dawn to sunset. The joke was that the Indios had a work ethic and the rest had a don't work ethic. They were a very simple, complicated people.

Clint was a multi-millionaire with houses in several places who stayed on the comarca most of the time with those he considered his people. He had a place here. It was that simple. He would go with Andres and Jorge today to harvest and dry cacao. He would work with them until around noon, come to the house to be with Tyna and have a meal, then return. He would come home at dusk, tired and content.

Nito came back with seven eggs in a small reed basket and put them on the table. "I'll be ready to go to work in a minute!" he said. He went inside.

Clint hugged Tyna and kissed her beautiful long shiny black hair. Nito would go with him for the morning. He had a job, along with several others from his age to about seven, of sorting the cacao and keeping it spread thin enough on the tarp that it would dry properly. In the afternoon he would help around the house and would study. Clint had some things that he brought to teach him English and numbers. He would probably go swimming later with the kids of the nearby village. They *did* play! They *were* children!

Nito came back out to say, "I'll fill the tank when I come back. I think it's low."

Clint had installed a large fiberglass water tank on the back porch roof so they could shower inside instead of going to the stream a couple times per day. The water for the tank was piped with PVC from a stream higher on the mountain. Nito would turn on the valve and watch until the tank was full, then turn it off. Clint was going to put a float valve in the tank, then considered that it was good for a child to have responsibilities. It made them know, as Nito had said, that they have a place in life.

He and Nito headed for the mountain and the cacao. It was going to be a good day.

Matilde was coming along the path when Tyna ran out to call to Clint that he had forgotten the chicha. She came to hand him a thermos.

Matilde looked closely at Tyna, smiled, and said,

"Girl."

"What?"

"You are pregnant. It will be a girl."

Tyna looked confused, then grinned. "I am?"

"Yes. It will be a healthy girl. You will name her ... that is a strange name ... Nicole."

Clint was standing open-mouthed. Nito cocked his head to the side. "I will have a baby sister?" Matilde smiled and nodded.

Matilde was a woman in her early forties. She was the local witch woman, which is not what it sounds. She would be the wise medicine woman. She was never wrong. She said she just knew. She didn't know how it worked, but work it did! They accepted it. Tyna would tell her mother and friends she was going to have a daughter named Nicole.

How did she know I like that name so much? Clint thought. He'd never mentioned it to anyone around there.

Clint and Nito went on to work. Matilde would stay to gossip with Tyna.

Clint came back at the end of the work day and he and Tyna went into the shower. Nito joined them. They teased and played awhile. Tyna served a delicious meal, starting with iguana soup, then chuletas (pork chops) breaded and fried, a mixed macaroni, potato, onion, carrot, broccoli, cauliflower, chayote and hardboiled egg salad and a lettuce, tomato and cucumber green salad. Maiz totillas. Fried bananas with a little honey. The only thing not from the finca and their own garden was the macaroni. Tyna even made the mayonnaise and the mustard for the mixed salad. Clint taught her to make vinegar from the pineapple they had all around the place and how to press out the corn oil. The chicha for tonight was milk, banana and pineapple. They even raised their own sugar. They had salt from the ocean.

This was paradise. This was how man was meant to live.

"Is the cacao done?" Tyna asked.

"Yeah. I'll help cut some nispero tomorrow I suppose. Basilio wants to build some things. We can go fishing the day after tomorrow. There are a lot of good lobster just north on the reef, and conch.

"Dano found a creek to the east where there are a lot of mussels. Maybe Nito can go with him and Jaime in the morning. Nispero is too heavy for me, much less Nito!"

"I think I'll stay home tomorrow. I have to dig the yampi and some yuca," Nito suggested. "It'll get too hard if we don't take some soon."

"That will be a good idea," Tyna said. "We can use some. I've been getting just what I need, but it does get hard if you don't dig it. Lana and Flora can come and we can dig up all of that by the wall. They'll want some handy. Flora's coming, anyway with sugar. The vainilla should be ready. It's been four months. It should only need a drop in a chicha."

"Hanna bought me a vainilla helado. That stuff from the mercado. It was blah," Nito said. "Why doesn't the vainilla from the mercado taste like the vainilla here?"

"Because it's artificial," Clint explained. "In real vanilla you get twenty or thirty different flavors. In the artificial you only get the one. I was amazed when I first tasted the real thing. All my life I loved vanilla shakes. When Dave fixed those he made with the vanilla he extracted it blew my mind!"

Tyna laughed and said a lot of things he knew in

life from that artificial culture were, as Nito said, blah. She started teasing and Clint started teasing. Nito laughed and said he was going to bed. They would get into that sex stuff. He didn't know whether he was looking forward to when he knew what it was about or not.

"You'll find what things you like in its own time," Clint said. "The chemicals in your body change when you're about twelve or thirteen."

"Or nine. Luis likes to talk about how he thinks Samuél is so handsome and so sexy. I think he would drop his pants and bend over in half a second if Samuél wanted him to!"

"He's gay. It's a little early to know, but he already knows some things he'll want," Tyna said. "Don't do anything with him you don't want to. I don't think you'll be gay."

Clint wasn't shocked. This was a normal kind of discussion among his people. They knew some were and some weren't. They believed everyone should have a place in that the same as they did in other things.

"I don't think the gringo will know anything. He was scratching his crotch because it itched or something and his mother said, real strict, not to play with himself. She looked at me and her face turned sort of darker. I said not to look at me! I wasn't going to play with him!"

Clint burst out laughing. Tyna got the giggles. "What did she say?" Tyna asked.

He shrugged. "Just something about nasty little pagans. I don't think they'll stay here long."

Nito went to bed. Tyna and Clint soon also went to bed.

In the morning Clint went into the forest with several others and two chain saws. The saws had special corundum tipped blades. Nispero would wear steel blades to nothing in almost no time.

There was a huge old tree that had fallen in a wind storm a couple of years ago. It was during the innundation when the stream had loosened the ground under it. It was probably a hundred ten feet before the large first branch. The tree was probably close to a thousand years old when it fell.

They cut a section from near the base about six meters long and cut a slab off of one side about three inches thick. It took more than an hour to cut the board out. One meter wide by two inches thick by six meters long. It would weigh well over eight hundred pounds. They made a slide of heliconia leaves and managed to turn it flat on them with levers made of ten foot poles. It was downhill at a fairly sharp angle to the stream, where it could be laid on a cayuca that was a little longer than the board and floated to the village. It was getting dark when they reached the village. Fourteen men came to carry it to the shed. It was already fairly cured, but they would cure it completely before using it. They would now put moisture on the parts that were drying too fast to keep it from warping and cracking. That process would take several months. The timber people from the cities would take such planks, run them through a planer and use them in days. They would warp and split. This one would remain flat and straight. The men would take fine silica sand on hides and sand the upper surface for hours until it was a shiny polished smooth board.

This was to be the counter in the new food preparation area where people who were working nearby would be served food. It was a community project. The women would prepare the food and serve it.

The rest of the section of log would be cut into four by fours and six by eights. They would be used for the frame and joists for the building, then softer and easier to work with wood would be used to finish it. Nothing affects nispero. The rest of the building would be replaced or repaired when necessary, but that frame would still be there in two hundred years.

Clint ran his hand across the plank and felt a proud sense of accomplishment. They'd done an excellent job!

The men who worked on the project went to the river and bathed, then went home. Nito had come looking for him at dusk and went back with him. Tyna caught him up on the day's happenings and he told her about the cutting. There were two large bags of yuca on the porch and one of yampi.

They went to bed a little early. Clint was tired. It was a good tired.

In the morning Basilio came to call while Clint was still in the shower. Tyna called for him to come in and make himself at home. There was coffee and she would cook up something for breakfast.

"I think this is what you would call an official visit," Basilio answered. "Omar has found a dead body in the ocean. He is bringing it to town. It was told to me by mountain calls so I know only very little. He did say it was not a natural death."

Clint knew that a lot of information could be relayed though the calls that men working and living in the mountains used. He came out and dressed. "I suppose this is what the omen was about," he said.

Nito came and stood there. Clint and Basilio had a fast cup of coffee while Tyna and Nito had avena. Tyna handed them each several boiled eggs and they set out for the town. Clint almost said that Nito couldn't go with them, but this was the comarca. Nito was Ngobe. He must experience such things, though Clint felt some trepidation. The Indio children knew that everyone died, that they would have to face death to know not to fear it.

They came onto the dock where Omar was just tying the cayuca. Several people were waiting. They helped take the body, wrapped in a tarp, out of the boat and laid it on the dock. Clint remarked that it was a very small body. It must be a child.

"Yes. A child," Omar said. "A gringo maybe. He was killed with a wire around his neck and thrown into the water. I found him near the reef when I dove for some conch. He was under and I did not see him before I went into the water."

He cut the small tie string and they unrolled the tarp. Omar had wrapped the body.

"It's Rami!" Nito said. "Why would he be out there? He was afraid to even go swimming!"

"He's no Panamanian, but he's also no gringo," Clint said.

"Nobody liked him, but they wouldn't kill him for that," Nito said. "You wanted to hit him in the mouth sometimes, but not really hurt him."

"There is something very odd and very strange here," Basilio said. "Who would kill a child, no matter how obnoxious? Why?"

"That's for sure a couple of sixty four thousand dollar questions," Clint answered.

"You never make any damned sense!" Basilio complained. "I think I know what you mean."

"It was an old TV show. You could win as much as sixty four thousand dollars by answering questions."

"It needs explanation at some other time and in some other place if at all," Basilio replied. "Take the body to the clinic, please."

They went to the clinic and called the doctor from Chiriqui Grande. He would be there in four hours.

"I think it would be the time to tell the mother," Basilio said a few minutes later. "Will you come with me?"

"Yes, but I don't want Nito to be there," Clint answered. "People who are in grief need as few strangers around as possible."

Nito and Basilio both agreed with that. Nito would go home and tell Tyna what had happened. Clint and Basilio would go to the house Rami's mother was renting to tell her her son was dead.

No one answered the door. Clint said he was afraid her body might be the next one found.

There was a thumping sound from inside. Clint didn't hesitate. He charged the door with his shoulder and it splintered from the lock.

The woman was gagged and tied to a chair. When she heard them she rocked it until it fell over. Clint sat her up and carefully removed the duct tape across her mouth.

"Rami!" she screamed. "What have they done to Rami! He is not going back! Stop them! Don't let them take him from this country! Please! For the mercy of Allah! Don't let them do this! He is only a boy!"

"I think there is a lot we must learn about this boy and his mother," Basilio said.

"You do like understatement, don't you?" Clint replied.

They untaped her and helped her stand. She went wobbly to the bed and sat there.

"Tell me," she said defeatedly. "They have already gone? They had a boat waiting? They have already taken him?

"How did they find us? I thought here they would not seek us. They could not know we were in Panamá. They could not know we were on the comarca.

"Who told them? How did they find us?

"He is Rami Ashirikar. He is a prince they will now make a monster of. His father resents that I was able to mother the only child he will ever have. He is old and of very low sperm count according to the doctors.

"Rami is the next sheik. His father is a monster. They will make one of him also. I know his destiny is to be sheik. I hoped to change that he would be a monster."

"When did they take him? Why did no one know?" Basilio asked.

"It was very late. No one was about. They came silently. They are trained. They took him and put me in the chair. They will answer to Allah for putting their hands on me!"

"I'm Clint Faraday. This is Basilio, the chief here. You are?" Clint asked.

"I am called Princess Sarita Shemenshi Al Shirikar. I used the name of Sara Shemberg here so they would think I am Jewish. No one from my country would ever want to be identified as a Jew!"

"Can you identify the ones who did this to you?" Basilio asked.

"No. They had their heads wrapped to only the eyes."

"I'm afraid I have to tell you something that is very difficult to say. Rami is dead," Basilio said, sadly.

She looked shocked, then said, "Why would ... how?"

"Garotted," Clint replied. "Then thrown in the ocean."

"So. Now Nadir will be sheik when Qanar dies. I cannot identify those who came here, but I can identify who sent them!

"Very well! My life is over. I will tell Qanar what has happened. I will say that Nadir will not live to be sheik!"

"Who is Qanar and who is Nadir you speak of?" Basilio asked.

"Qanar is the sheik, Rami's father. Nadir is his brother."

She went to a drawer and took out a roaming cell phone. She punched a number and spoke in a foreign language for a moment, at one time becoming extremely imperious and demanding. After a couple more minutes she was transferred to another person, then to another, finally to someone she called "Qanar." Clint assumed that was her husband, the sheik. She mentioned "Nadir" several times.

She rang off and turned to Clint and Basilio. "Nadir will not survive this hour. What am I to do now?"

"We will not molest you for awhile," Basilio promised. "Will you be safe here?"

"I will be safe nowhere. That is a relative term. I will be returned."

"No. Not if you do not wish to be returned," Basilio promised. "This is the comarca. I am law here."

"They will come for me. I don't think you can stop them."

"I think we can," Clint said. "There's a lot they and you don't know about my people.

"I believe you were doing what you did for the good of that boy. I'll arrange something where you'll be safe, then I'm going after them. They may be able to do this kind of crap wherever you came from, but this ain't wherever you came from.

"Basilio, can you get her to Quebrada Tula?"

"Yes."

"And in a way they won't know she's gone?"

"Yes."

"Then let's do that!"

They made arrangements for Sara to be taken to Clint's place near Quebrada Tula, also on the comarca. No one would find her there.

He thought of something and said, "Don't take that cell phone with you. It has an automatic GPS beacon attached for the signal to find you anywhere on the planet. It's probably how they found you here. If the phone's here, they'll assume you're here."

"They must silence me before I am able to contact Qanar. I have already contacted Qanar."

"They may know you used the phone. They

won't know who you called. They might think you called someone here to have them stopped."

"But they will know when Nadir dies."

"No. They'll know when he dies, but not why he died. Call Qanar again."

"Does he speak Spanish?"

"No. He speaks English."

Clint handed her his phone. He said not to use hers. She called. The time was a lot less. She spoke for a minute with Qanar, then handed the phone to Clint.

"Sheik? I'm Clint Faraday. We know what happened and we can figure what will happen to your brother. It's important that his operatives here don't know you had anything to do with that. Do you understand?"

"No. Why would I care?"

"They killed your son. They are trained. They can escape you. They can't escape me if they don't know that you know."

There was a long pause. "What you say may well be true. Nadir had an accident. He got drunk and fell into the garden under his balcony. It is very sad that there was an asp in the garden. The family is in deep grief." He hung up.

"Okay. We have some time. Let's get you out of here and leave your phone. They'll assume the last thing you'd do is call Qanar. Rami will simply have disappeared somewhere when Qanar dies.

"When they find Nadir is dead they'll know they have to silence you. You'll be the only link to Nadir and his child killers."

She nodded and began packing some things. She had to have at least five million dollars worth of jewelry with her. She saw Clint looking at it.

"It is only for security. I do not wear jewelry. I would not parade my wealth in front of the poor, like so many."

They soon took Sara out and to the community building. Basilio had the women dress her in the dresses they wore and darken her skin and hair. She was soon loaded onto a cayuca to go to Chiriqui Grande with yucca, yampi and cacao. She would be met there by a family and taken by bus to Chiriqui where she would take a bus to Soloy, then go by horse to Quebrada Tula.

When they came to the dock Clint stood looking for them to bring her. Basilio laughed. Matilde introduced an old woman as Sara Salvaje. It was Sara. Clint saw the disguise was at least as good as some he'd used.

When they were gone Clint went back into town and talked with Basilio awhile, then went home to spend the rest of the day with Tyna and Nito. Tonight, he was going to be in Sara's house. This was the kind of thing that would have to happen fast. If they found that Nadir was dead and the body had been found, they would panic. Clint didn't doubt that Nadir had died from being bitten by an asp. He had probably run around in a room full of them trying to avoid being bitten.

At dusk he went to the town. The boat that took Sara to Chiriqui Grande was back. Emilio, the owner, said Sara had seen three men in Chiriqui Grande who must have been the ones who killed Rami. She had started to go after them with a knife. They didn't see her until the other women stopped her. They were holding her. One of the women told one of the evil men that she was prone to strange attacks. She would be alright in a minute. They got her away. She was on the way to Soloy.

Clint went to talk with his friends for awhile and to spend the whole evening talking and joking. Enrique, a gay man from Norteño, decided he would spend the night with Clint in Sara's house. Clint said that he would spend one boring night because he was still Tyna's one and only.

"I'm not trying to take you! I just want to borrow you!"

They joked. Clint finally went to the house and checked his traps. No one had been there. He went to the bedroom and sacked out.

Nothing happened. He went to the dock in the morning. Dario said a boat had come past twice, once heading east and once heading west. It did not come to the dock

He went home and spent the entire day helping Samuél clear a place to grow frijoles. It would be a patch with four kinds of the beans that was big enough to supply them to everyone. He spent until after dark with Tyna and Nito, then went back to Sara's where he spent another night with nothing.

The next day he went fishing with Omar. He returned home about three and spent the rest of the day with Nito and Tyna. That night would be the last one he would spend there. They would come before this if they were coming. Someone was sneaking around at three in the morning. He waited until the traps showed someone was in the house. He carefully moved to behind the bedroom door. It slowly opened and someone crept silently toward the bed. Clint turned the flashlight on him and said, "Move and die!"

He froze. Clint kept the light in his eyes and moved out to stand just behind the door. A hand appeared with a pistol. He hit the arm with the flashlight. Hard. There was a shot into the floor.

There was a commotion outside and the sounds of a struggle. Clint moved to tell the one who had dropped the pistol to come slowly into the room and to stand beside his buddy. A moment later, two Indios came in with a man between them.

"Sit them on the side of the bed. All of them," Clint suggested. "We'll see what they have to say for themselves."

They said they wouldn't be saying anything to anyone until they had a lawyer present.

"What? You think this is the US?" Clint asked. "They don't have any such law here! If Panamá did, you're on the Comarca Ngobe Bugle, where Panamanian law doesn't apply.

"You heard about Nadir's accident?"

"Yes, Mr. Faraday, I did. I caused it. I am Qanar Ashirikar. The persons responsible for the death of my son are no more a consideration.

"Where is Sarita?"

"Maybe Costa Rica, maybe Nicaragua, by now. Maybe Colombia, maybe Peru or Ecuador. A lot of people are moving to Ecuador I hear."

"So. I know five places she will not be found. I will find her."

"Why?"

"She took my son away."

"She took him away to try to save him."

"He was to be next sheik."

"She understood that. She just didn't want him to be like you."

"That is truth? She would not keep him from

knowing he was to be sheik?"

"She said it was his destiny."

"Then I misjudged her."

"This isn't the best time or situation to learn that!"

"Far too true. I am in a country I do not know nor understand, among a group of people I do not know nor understand. They have put their hands on me, which would lose them those hands at home."

"Lovely place. Lovely society. I'm damned glad it's not here."

"Well, I will go. I will find Sarita. If what you say is true there will be no further action against her except the divorce. I wait to divorce her until I know that truth."

"You aren't going anywhere until we find a truth or two," Basilio, who had been by the door for the past two or three minutes, said. He spoke excellent English. "You will first have to answer for disrupting our lives like this. Had you come in the daytime and asked about the lady we would have told you she is gone. That would be the honorable way. You chose this dishonorable way.

"Clint, this is no longer in your charge. I am chief. I declare this is now to the council."

Clint nodded. Basilio was doing that to make sure there wouldn't be retaliation against Clint or his family.

"He threatened to cut the hands off of anyone who touched him. I think you should know that."

"I see. Perhaps we should cut the feet off of anyone who sneaks around the comarca after, say, midnight?"

"Sounds fair."

Qanar said, "I get the point. It's what we would do at home. I swear that no action will be taken against any of you. It isn't easy to remember that I'm not a sheik here."

"You're a sheik here, too. The problem for you is that nobody here gives a happy damned shit!" Clint replied and grinned. Qanar let a small grin flash across his face.

"I want only two of the jewelry items Sarita has taken. They are from my mother and her mother and her mother. The rest mean nothing. They are only jewels like millions of others."

"They were to be given to the next sheik?" Clint remembered something from another case.

"Yes."

"There can be no next sheik without those jewels?"

"Of course there can. And will be. They are not a part of the proof of power. They are personal heirlooms."

"If I get them for you, you will leave everyone

here alone? Including Princess Sarita? This on your honor?"

"This I swear on my honor."

Clint nodded and went outside. He called Sara on the phone he'd gotten for her and explained about what had happened.

"He is more faults than wellnesses, but he is very much honorable to his words. If he said he will do something on his honor, he will do it."

"Do you know which jewels he wants?"

"No. I took them all from the jewel case in his rooms."

Clint stepped back inside and asked which of the jewels he wanted.

"The large emerald with six rubies around in the heavy gold setting and the large sapphire with the eleven diamonds. If she will grant, I'd like the red opal with the nine pearls on the chain. That is personal."

Clint stepped out and told her. She said they weren't among her favorites anyway. They were ostentatious and she was not. She would get them to David as soon as she could.

"I'll contact a good friend who will bring them to David. He can say they arrived at his place in Panamá City by courier and he doesn't know where they came from."

He then called a friend in Soloy who would have

the jewels in David the following day, remembering that this was four o'clock in the morning of today.

"Basilio, we can take this man's word of honor. We can go to David. The jewels will be delivered there tomorrow afternoon."

"All I ever had to do was ask?" Qanar asked, incredulous.

"Certainly. We have no use for jewels," Basilio replied.

"Well. I can have everything except an heir."

"Let's talk to someone in the morning," Clint suggested. "Well, in a couple of hours. This *is* the morning."

They agreed. Qanar would wait on his boat and take Clint to Chiriqui Grande where he would have a helicopter to take them to David.

At about seven o'clock Clint and Qanar went to call at a small neat cabin near the beach in town. Matilde answered the door. Clint said he wanted to know if she knew a way that Qanar could father a child. He explained. She invited them in.

She talked to Qanar and placed a piece of mother of pearl on his arm and told him not to move. After the shell stayed there for about a minute she said he could have a child. His only problem was that there were natural things that weren't in his diet. She went around the house looking for things. She soon came back with a sack of seeds. She said he was to find a good woman to be the mother and was to take one of the black seeds one of the gray seeds and one of the speckled seeds with each meal for a week, then was to try to father the child until the seeds were gone or until there was a child.

"And Clint. Tell him he is to raise the child to be a human being, not a thing such as he has become."

Clint relayed the message. Qanar started to get indignant, thought a moment, and thanked her for her honesty and for what she had done for his country. He could look at himself through other eyes here. He saw that she was right.

They went to the waiting boat. Tyna sent Nito with some clothes and items and said to be home again soon. She had enough nights with only Nito and Nicole in the room with her. Clint clung to Nito for a few minutes, then they were on the way to Chiriqui Grande.

"You are a fine father. Your son is an adult already, but still a child. I see that in many here. You must be very proud. I must admit Rami was not one to be proud of. It was my fault."

"You can't know."

He nodded. They watched the ocean until the fast boat came into Chiriqui Grande. The waiting car took them to the little airport. Qanar said to take the boat to the canal and they would meet in three days. He and Clint headed for David.

Clint showed him around the city. He said he felt safe, which is something else he had never really known. No one was trying to assassinate him here!

"They don't care who you are somewhere else here," Clint explained. "Here, you're that fat man in the expensive suit. You must be a lawyer."

He roared in laughter. "Picture me a lawyer!"

It wasn't really unpleasant after Qanar learned that he wasn't giving any orders here. The jewels arrived at a little after seven. Qanar decided he would stay there in David another day, then head home. Clint had the helicopter take him directly home. Qanar insisted he was paying for it. If he actually was able to father a child he was going to make Clint a celebrity and Matilde a princess.

"We're both Ngobe. We don't want to be anything less," Clint replied.

"I, as the saying in California went, envy the hell out of you!" They parted, if not friends, at least not enemies.

Clint arrived at his place just before seven the following morning. Nito ran to the chopper and Tyna came to call to the pilot that she had plenty of food and it was time for breakfast. He went in and they chatted awhile and had a great breakfast of several types of melon, papaya, pineapple with a thick piece of pork on cornbread with gravy.

He spent the morning with Tyna and Nito and the afternoon helping build a house for a couple who were just married. The night was spent with his family. The next morning he went to help cut stringers and runners from the nispero. The next day he went fishing with Omar.

Things were back to idyllic! Sara had gone back to a place in the Mediterranean where she had relatives.

A month and four days later Clint got a call from Qanar. "Prince Clint, please inform Princess Matilde that I am to be a father in nine months! You people are amazing! Hundreds of doctors and millions of dollars and a wise woman in an Indian village gives me the cure for nothing!"

"It's not for nothing. Nothing ever is. You have to remember how you promised to raise the heir. If you were here, she would be able to tell you at a glance if the baby will be male or female. She's never wrong."

They chatted like old friends for a few minutes, then rang off. Maybe he had learned a lesson and would raise an heir who wasn't, as Sara said, a monster. The world could use a few less monsters in positions of power. Read a newspaper, watch

TV. You can't get around the facts. The hman race was in sharp decline in some areas.

<u>Baby Boom</u>

Clint answered the phone two days later. Qanar was having a second and third baby. He was out of seeds, but didn't care. One was almost certain to be a boy. If it was number two or three, which would become sheik was a matter of minutes! While he didn't have to select the oldest son, it was the way it had been for generations.

Clint went to work with Basilio on the comida house. The nispero had cured perfectly and the wood shone like cherry wood he had seen on a bar in Tampa years ago. The framework for the house was done and the wood for the sides was ready to install. They had put in the floor the day before. The roof would be a special fiberglass that would look like the palm fronds they had originally planned on using. Clint asked where it came from.

"Remember that sheik? Qanar?

"Well, he called to ask me to translate for Matilde. He said she was a princess and could have a palace anywhere she wanted it in the world. She said she was in the only place in the world suited to her. He said she could have a palace here. She said it was a truly horrible idea. They laughed. He said his daughter, the first one born, was to be Matilde, that she had to accept some kind of gift for what she had done. She would get a jewel worth ten million dollars. She said that was asother horrible an idea, but she did know of one thing he could do. We were building a comida house and the frond top would have bugs. Maybe enough zinc for it?

"He said they wanted palm fronds, they would have palm fronds. He would have a roof designed that would be perfect and would look like palm fronds.

"Two men came here from Arabia. They saw what we wanted. They made the roof. They are real palm fronds and will always be green. They are placed exactly as we wanted them, then they made the acrylic coating. It is heavy, but that is good because the nispero will support more weight than we could get up there. It is all in one piece. They had a helicopter come to lift it onto the posts. It fit exactly! It was like something we Ngobe would make!

"It will need repairs in about sixty years."

Matilde came to watch them place the perfect boards for the walls. "Greetings, Princess Matilde!" Clint called.

"And to you, Prince Clint!" They both giggled. Matilde said that she would like to speak with Clint at the midday break and went on to her house.

At noon (or thereabout) Clint went to her house and sat on the porch with her. She said there was something very wrong. It was something from the past that was coming to haunt them now. She didn't know what it was, but someone very evil was involved. Someone was planning to kill another child. Maybe more than one. Someone was planning to kill a king. It didn't make sense to her. It was someone they both knew, but didn't know.

Clint thought. Matilde was never wrong. He was concerned that she wasn't this time.

"We'll have to wait and see," Clint suggested. "Is it immediate?"

"Yes. We can't wait, but we have no way to know who or where.

"Clint, there are people who are raised to be decepters. They are taken as very small children and taught carefully the ways of being believed. Usually it is the father or mother who create these ... things. They are not people. They know only one emotion, often greed. They are very few, but are among us. We can't detect them even with my talent. Perhaps we can feel an ... emptiness. They are skilled in being around when there are other strong emotions close to hide that they have none."

He went back to work, wondering. The only king he knew was Qanar. It must be that someone was planning to kill his children. Clint called him and told him what Matilde had said. He was worried.

"Qanar, I would think one of your wives was planning to kill the children of the others, but we don't know any of them. If it's about you, we ... it would have to be Sarita. Tell me all you know about her."

"She can't do anything to us here from there," he answered.

"Qanar, she's somewhere in the Mediterranean! She isn't here!"

"Then she is close. I can't begin to think what she might plan.

"She is the daughter of a minor dignitary in Saudi Arabia. We met and made the agreement about an heir. I was able to father Rami with her, but my condition had gotten so bad I would not be able to father another child. I did not approve of the way she was raising my son and had him removed from her direct care. She ran away with him. We found her again, there.

"Clint, if she is here she can't do anything to anyone there. That works both ways. I would like to have my wives and heirs there until we know what is happening. I feel they will be safe there.

"Clint, it occurs for the first time what Ishmael

meant when he was ... disposed of there. He was one who was with the killers of Rami.

"He said Nadir was not the one. That's all. I didn't know what he was talking about. I think perhaps I do now. I think that's why they did not immediately go to Cusapín to silence her."

"What could she have been up to?"

"Clint, I did not view Rami's body...?"

Clint thought about that one. "Qanar, send a DNA chart on you to Chiriqui Grande as soon as possible! The doctor will have samples from Rami. It's standard anymore!"

They soon rang off. Clint sat back. He thought a little more and called a friend in Quebrada Tula.

Then he went back to work.

The doctor in Chiriqui Grande called and asked what the DNA chart was about. It had come in on the computer under his name.

"Doc, check that against the chart on that Rami kid who was killed here. Call me when you have anything, match or not."

"It's here on the computer. I can bring it up and check."

There was a short pause. "Hmm. Less than four percent. That they are in any way related is one chance in four billion."

"Thanks, Doc." He rang off and called Qanar. "He wasn't your son. Who was he?"

"I don't know. I wonder where my son is."

"He's not born yet is my guess."

"There was a son."

"Possibly, but were you the father? Consider your medical condition at the time. Maybe that's why she had to get rid of ... no. There was no family match."

"To her?"

"I don't have her DNA."

"I don't doubt that we do. I'll have it sent."

Clint waited. An hour and a half later Doc called and said there was no match on that one to any of the others. What was going on?

"I wish to holy hell I knew!"

He rang off and went back to work. He went home at about four and played with his family. Osorio called from Tula to say he couldn't find anything in the house. He checked the water tank like Clint said and there was something in it. A big bottle.

"What was in the bottle?"

"A cell phone and a spring and a rock and a lot of white powder. There is no signal for that kind of phone here."

"Put it in the bodega and lock it, please. It's supposed to kill off my whole family or somebody else's. Probably both."

Clint hung up and thought. The lady was very

convincing and very clever. He would make her think he was going to now do exactly what she planned on him doing. He called Qanar again and explained.

He waited four days until the wives arrived. He sent them with some Indio friends to Buabidi, across the comarca. He went to Quebrada Tula. Qanar said he had the word out that his pregnant wives were on vacation in an undisclosed place where they would be safe until his progeny were delivered.

After a few minutes of thought Clint called Tyna and asked that she and Nito join the wives of Qanar. Nito knew too much. She agreed.

Two nights later, just before dinnertime, the bottle as much as exploded. It was inside a drum. The powder went everywhere. The top wasn't tight on the drum and they could smell cyanide. Clint quickly tightened the cap. He called Qanar, who said he was getting used to being awakened at any odd time by Clint.

"What it was simple. A big jar of sodium cyanide. A spring with a rock on one end. The spring was compressed and the rock was about an inch from the glass. A cell phone set to vibrate. A small lever against the phone that moved a wire. It worked like an old-fashioned rat trap. The jar was shattered. There was a small vial with a rubber cap that was pulled out when the rock was released. Sulfuric acid. Clever and easy. A big cloud of cyanide gas would cover the house and pour right into the back door. No one would live more than seconds in the house."

"It is frightening. What is next?"

"You have to die, she comes up with your son, he becomes sheik, she lives in luxury for the rest of her life. I imagine her father or mother or both would share that luxury."

"She will be found. This must not be allowed to continue a moment more."

"You got that right!"

"Do you have any suggestions, my friend?"

"If you can find how she plans to get rid of you, let her think it was successful."

"Most certainly!"

Clint went into Quebrada Tula to find that the few people who had celulars reported that they all rang at once earlier. What did Clint do?

"I took away the reason for them to ring."

He arranged for the big drum of cyanide to be neutralized. A nitrite compound would be sent from David with instructions on how to use it.

Clint headed for Soloy. He could move in any direction there.

He got a call. "Clint? Qanar. A man who looked much like me happened to be riding in one of my cars on the desert when the car was hit with what was described as being a G to G missile. That information was just released to the international press. I have discovered that Sarita recently left the Mediterranean. She has been gone for four and a half days. Perhaps she is again there."

"We'll know very soon. I wonder what her story will be. It should be a dilly!"

"Perhaps we shall be able to point out the flaws, would you say?"

"Something like that."

"Clint, how would she know that the cyanide worked there? Would she not have a way to be sure? If she moves prematurely all will be lost."

"If it worked totally, there would be nothing. If it didn't work, someone would have reported it. No one reported anything."

"Ah! Clever and stupid at the same time. If no one was there, nothing would be reported. Things will seem to always have happened in her favor. She is very smart and very lucky."

"No. Her original plan went to hell because of Matilde. You were to live a few days or weeks after you had gotten rid of Nadir. You suddenly had heirs. She had to make another plan, but it could be based on the original. Remember; she doesn't know we're onto her!"

"Yes. I have thought much about this. I think she would know about DNA. I think I know why Nadir was necessarily removed. I think he was not innocent in this, as I know he was far from innocent in other intrigues."

"I thought that was possible. There should be enough of a match that they can't definitely say he isn't your child."

"And Nadir is no longer where he would be the next in line to become sheik. He was used, then discarded. She is without a soul, Clint. She need not fear perdition."

"I tend to agree."

They chatted about it for half an hour more.

Clint then waited. There wasn't anything else to do. The next move was Sarita's.

The move came very early the next day when Sarita Shemsenshi Al Ashirikar came from where she had been hiding from assassins in an undisclosed location in The Darien, Panamá. No nearer location would be given because she had Sheik Qanar Ashirikar's son with her. Sarita admitted that she had taken the son away from the influence of the sheik because hc *Was a total, evil, vile monster who would have raised the boy to be like him. He was not the benevolent leader his people were led to believe.*

People will try to claim that I am another of the schemers who wish to grab the power. I ask that a DNA test of the family traits be matched to the test of the boy. In today's world we can prove things that were impossible to prove in the past, thanks be to Allah!

Arrangements will be made to return the new sheik when it is shown to do so would be safe.

It has been reported that the sheik has fathered other children very recently, that his doctors were amazed that an ancient fertility potion seemed to have worked. Not only one, but three wives were pregnant. The princess said that it didn't matter, as her son is the eldest. All the semi-siblings would be treated as princes and princesses as was custom.

In other news....

Clint grinned and called Qanar, who said all communication from the compound is held in abeyance for a grieving period.

"I notice how carefully she wanted it to be family DNA traits, not my personal DNA traits."

"Well, it will be questionable if Allah would approve of desecrating your body by taking a sample directly. Or something."

"True. Well? We will wait until she produces Nadir's son to act?"

"Yeah. You can have been in an opium stupor for the past week or so and had no idea! Aren't you glad the old sheik names his next in line, that it is *not* the old English system of the eldest inheriting where you are?"

"I was in an opium stupor? Would that it were true!"

They laughed and joked for awhile. Clint called Basilio, who said some men were asking about Tyna and Nito. They were told that they were with some women from the Far East somewhere and would return in a week or so.

Clint went to the bus. He would go to Panamá City to speak with the Princess Sarita in person.

He called Tyna and spoke with her and Nito until the bus came to take him to Boca Morito, where he would get the bus to Panamá City.

A friend who watched the bus stop said that a man came who wanted to go to Quebrada Tula. He was told that no foreigners could go there for twenty eight days, until the next full of the moon, because of the traditional festival of prediction. The man said there were already foreigners there he wanted to visit. He was told there may be, but they were not in the town and would not be allowed in the town.

"The man said he wanted to go to where they were, not the town. I told him he couldn't go anywhere in the area without going first to the town. He would not be allowed to go to the town. Come back and visit in twenty eight days. He said that he would then send a message for them. Could it be delivered? I said yes. In twenty eight days."

"What if he had pointed out that it isn't the full of the moon?"

"I would have told him that we have our own calendar here, thank you very much!"

Clint grinned and hugged Salvatore and got on the bus. Sarita's luck was phenomenal! She had twenty eight days to solidify her position!

The trip to the city was mostly uneventful. Clint chatted with people on the bus and slept. When he got there he checked into a hotel and called a friend in the police. Mario agreed to go along with him after he laid the whole thing out for him.

"You've seen the boy? They have the DNA sample? Sara's where you can grab her?"

"Yes, but there may be a problem. She *is* a princess. She can claim diplomatic immunity."

"Did she use a diplomatic passport?"

"No. She used one in the name of Sara Mary Shemberg."

"Then she admits to using a false passport, it's not diplomatic. She's a criminal for that little fact. She can be prosecuted at our discretion."

"Technically, yes. Actually, no. She's already bribed the right person. I understand a certain judge's wife is newly sporting a necklace worth more than fifty thousand."

"Welcome to Panamá!"

"It turns your stomach! What did she do?"

"Other than kill a three year old boy and some other people and try to kill the other wives and heirs of the sheik, not too much – we know of."

"Lovely lady. She can make you really sorry for her, the woman who has taken a small child away from an evil monster and has been hiding him to keep him safe."

"Yeah. I've heard it."

"We can go talk with her. Maybe it will be a shock to have you here."

"The lady can't be shocked nearlyso easily. She'll have a story."

Clint made a fast call to Qanar. He told him to be ready.

They headed for the Europa and to the plush penthouse suites where she was holding a press conference. When they came in the door across the room from her she hardly reacted. They let her finish with her story about how she had to sneak away from the compound with her son with the help of the brother of the sheik, who was since murdered in cold blood by the sheik for aiding her.

When she finished and the press people were led out Clint and Mario went to her. She smirked at Clint and said, "Well, Mr. Faraday! It seems I owe you an explanation!

"I had to try to hide there in Cusapín with the substitute child because we feared that exactly what happened would happen. I couldn't tell you about Rami because I knew there was no one on this Earth I could trust and I didn't know you.

"I think Rami will be safe now that Qanar is dead. The DNA will prove my son is the rightful heir."

"What in the world makes you think Sheik Qanar is dead?" Mario asked. "The DNA shows the child could be his by a ratio of one to twenty six. It shows the DNA of a brother, Nadir, was it Clint? is a one in one chance of being the father."

"So? Nadir would be the sheik if there was no other heir. Rami would become sheik through that succession."

"No," Clint said. "Qanar would have to die before Nadir for that to happen. He can select anyone in his family to become next sheik. He selected the first son born. He has three pregnant wives. He can change that anytime he chooses."

"But he can't choose much when he's dead," she said, haughtily.

"We'll worry about that point when he's dead," Mario said. "You have to answer to the courts why that other child was sacrificed in this stupid plot."

"I don't have to answer to your courts for anything! I'm a princess and have been declared by your courts to be immune to prosecution!"

"I said 'the courts,' not our courts. Sheik Qanar can withdraw your immunity, then it may be our courts. We prefer that you be sent back there for his courts to handle. We don't need the expense or headaches."

"I will return with the new sheik. I'll not worry about his courts."

"There is no new sheik. Get that through your head. Qanar will handle it, himself," Clint said.

"There was a press release about his car being blown up. The simple fact is that he wasn't in the car."

He held up his cell phone, which had been on. Qanar was at the other end.

"That right, Qanar?"

"Yes, my good friend, that is right," Qanar replied. The phone was on speaker. Sarita showed a slight fear, then said he couldn't have her deported. She had the legal papers from the highest court here in Panamá."

"And?" Qanar asked. She was silent.

"Tell them the whole story and I will allow you to return to Saudi Arabia and your family. What you did has already exposed a scheming brother and some schemers in the guard. If we find who the parents of the boy you had killed are we will allow them to pursue charges through the courts of wherever.

"This is on the condition that you are truthful, as alien as that concept is to you. There is nothing you have done since that would negate the terms. You are not to try anymore silly plots against my family or myself, of course. I will listen and will know if it is, indeed, the truth you are relating, not another evil fairy tale."

She shook her head.

"You didn't get the wives," Clint said. "We

expected that."

She sighed. "Very well.

"The whole thing was started by Nadir. He...."

"She is lying in her first sentence. It started before she ever met Nadir."

She stared at the phone.

"It started when I was born, okay? It was my mother's idea to use it on my father, but I was a daughter and another wife had a first son. She trained me to do what she was planning. I would then make her a royal. I was trained to never allow anyone to know my true feelings to the point where I don't have feelings.

"The doctors said you would not have children except through rare accident of nature.

"We have DNA now. It is used to identify persons exactly as to their parentage and such. I studied genetics on line and learned about odds and chances. If the father was a close relative, the charts could be interpreted.

"I met Nadir. He was planning a coup that could not work. I enticed him to try my plan. He was close enough to where the DNA match would show a close relative if not father. Add to that the fact that Nadir would be the next sheik if Qanar died first. If they were both dead, the son would be the next sheik anyhow.

"Nadir fathered the boy. We knew Qanar would

discover the truth if we were there. I made up the story about him being a monster I felt I had to get the boy away from. I also knew he would find us very quickly. He has many resources.

"It was Nadir's idea to have a substitute son. He found the boy a year ago and we raised him to think he was Rami. I knew I would have to draw attention to the boy without seeming to. I spoiled him completely in the eyes of others. The real Rami is quiet and very easy to raise by the Ramones, the family in The Darien who kept him. I went to Cusapín with the substitute boy where he made us obvious, as planned.

"It was time for the next step in our plan. The boy would be used to divert attention. Qanar would become involved naturally when something happened to the boy. He would become vulnerable to attack by Nadir, who was now the one calling the steps. He had taken it from me.

"The boy was disposed of. He was no longer of use. Qanar was contacted.

"Nadir had spoken with me two nights before and was giving me orders. It was my plan and he was simply taking it from me. He was going to see that Qanar became deeply depressed when the last chance for having a son was gone and that he committed suicide. That would leave him sheik. I would already have the heir. He would marry his brother's four wives. That is common practice.

"I knew it would never happen. He was going to be sheik and he wasn't going to have any son around to knock him off and become sheik.

"I had a way to stop that! I let it accidentally become known that Nadir was behind the killing of the boy! Qanar would handle that the way those things are always handled. You succeed and live or fail and die. He would fail and die!

"Now I was in control again. Nadir was gone. The boy was gone. All I had to do was get rid of Qanar and I could come forward with the son who I had hidden in Panamá.

"There were several in the palace guard who would be glad to do something that would mean they advanced in rank and reward. Nadir was using them. Three have been taken care of here. There are two others here and two more in the palace. I imagine Qanar has found them now and that they are no more.

"I will not be able to go to Saudi Arabia."

"Why not?" Clint asked.

"Because she used the boy and discarded him, she used Nadir and discarded him, she used the guard and discarded them. Now she has failed," Qanar replied.

"And?"

"The plan was her mother's. She was being used.

She has failed. She will be discarded.

"Clint, send the boy, Rami, here to me. It is through no scheme or manipulation of his that he is in the situation he finds himself. I swear on my honor to raise him well and to not take action against him. He is innocent in this. Possibly the only one who has claim to that."

"Okay. I'll talk with you later." He rang off.

"Well! Choose a place!" Mario said to Sarita.

"A place?"

"You are not staying in Panamá."

"I know a place in the Mediterranean. I can go there."

"Very well. You leave tomorrow.

"Well, Clint! The amazing Faraday has again solved the case to where Panamá does not find it necessary to house, clothe and feed anyone for many years. You become adept at it.

"You will now go back to Cusapín?"

"No. I've never been to Buabidi. As a Ngobe I think I should see the place. I'll stay a little, then go back to Cusapín."

They went out as the two officers at her door went in to see she was ready for a flight out in the morning. She would become someone else's problem. If Qanar could find the parents of the dead boy they would be given the options. He was probably a boy who was sold as a baby. That, sadly, wasn't a rare thing in that area of the world.

Clint took care of what was left in the city and caught a bus to Buabidi. He found the place to be interesting and not what he expected in the, as it were, capital of the comarca. He had a good time. The wives of Qanar were a new kind of thing for all of them. He expected something quite a bit different there, but found they were reasonably content with their lot. They were interested in the way the children were raised on the comarca and were learning. Nito was a big hit with them. He had made a lot of friends with the local children his age. Tyna was a hit with everyone everywhere they went.

They stayed two weeks. Qanar wanted to be absolutely certain his wives were safe. He was coming, personally, to take them back home in his private plane. He came early. He would have two days in the town to learn about how others lived. He knew something about the Latina lifestyle and wanted to learn about the Indigenos. He was impressed with them when he was there before. He told Clint that he would give him a hundred million dollars for his beautiful wife. Clint laughed and said he wasn't about to sell her at discount. A hundred billion and he might think it over.

Qanar was liked by the people. They said he was

a good man. He had responsibility and was expected to protect his family. That is what a man does. They planned to kill his family. He had every right and duty to kill them first.

Qanar and the women were on a plane home. Clint and family were on a bus home. Sarita was somewhere in the Mediterranean.

Life could be good if you let it. Nito had a few gifts from Qanar. He would be covered with them if Clint hadn't explained that it wasn't good for a child to have too much. Qanar had spoken with the elders long and studiously. He bought a lot of things that were to be dispensed by Nito to his friends in Cusapín. The one special gift was his alone. It was a beautifully woven leather belt that Qanar made himself. It had a silver and turquoise buckle.

Qanar said the gift wasn't worth much money. He was impressed when Nito said it was worth more than any money could buy. Nito gave him a necklace made from small matched shells and a large shark's tooth. He agreed the gift was the most valuable one he had ever received.

"I think I learn much from the Ngobe. I have learned that price has nothing to do with value. This was a thing made with care by a small child. It was made for me alone.

"It is true. I have received gifts worth ... no. With

a *price* of many millions of dollars. The gift that is worth most to me is this one. It is from someone who gave it to me because he cares about me. Others have cost much more, but they have no worth, no value."

Nito hugged him and said the belt was the best gift he ever got and that he would keep it always.

When they reached Chiriqui Grande they loaded all the things they had into Clint's boat and headed to Cusapín. They had three passengers who were going there, so they took them along. Basilio met them and helped carry some things to the house. They settled in and Clint and Nito went into town. Tyna said she had enough of towns for awhile and stayed at the house. Nito took several of the gifts to give to friends. Some of them were silver and turquoise trinkets Qanar had made. He liked to work with turquoise. He also could work silver in a very artistic way.

Life was back to normal in two days. It was like they never left.

It had been almost five months since the sheik had come into Clint's life. Nicole Faraday S. was born just a week ago. Clint was working with Salvatore in the frijole garden. Nito was helping the clam fisherman in town. The world was drifting along as usual. They didn't know much about what was happening outside the comarca and didn't care.

Clint's phone had four uncompleted calls on it when he got home. He called Qanar.

"Clint, I wish to inform the world that my son, Omar Ahmed Asirikar, was born last night. He is healthy and complete. My other two children are to be born within four days.

"I did not name Omar after my great grandfather, as people believe. I named him after that good strong honest man there who fishes.

"I received the notice about your daughter like this. You called me to tell me. I like the custom. It is because we are friends, so formal messages are out of place between us.

"You and your family are well, I hope?"

"Better than we have any right to be. Most things are always – well, almost always – smooth and tranquil here on the comarca.

"Matilde says to tell you all your children will be healthy. Don't spoil them. Let them know they are people and that they have a place."

"I have learned that. Rami is doing well in school. I feel very close to him and he learned much while living with the people in The Darien. He has learned to think as an individual at four years."

"Here's Nito. He wants to say hello to you." Clint handed the phone to Nito and they chatted for a few minutes. Tyna talked a few minutes, then Clint talked again.

"Oh! Yes," Qanar said after a short while. "Sarita went to a small island some miles from here. She began to interfere in politics, trying to get a man she was living with elected – they are experimenting with democracy there – as mayor or something. She tried to bribe a woman who is in charge of a voting precinct to record enough votes for her paramour to win. The result was that he was disqualified and she will serve a term in women's prison. The sad thing is that he would have most likely won the election if she hadn't done that."

"She is what she is. It may not be her fault, but she is what she is."

"That sounds almost as wise as Nito sounds at

times! It is very true."

They talked for most of an hour more. Qanar called every week or ten days and would continue to do so. He said he could simply talk. He didn't have to be careful that he would offend someone who needed offending.

Four days later Clint got the announcement that both other babies had been born. Two beautiful girls, Tyna and Tabitha.

Clint and Qanar would remain friends for years. They both could feel it. One day Qanar called and said he was bored and would maybe bring his wives to Panamá for a vacation. They all wanted to go back to see the friends they'd made on the comarca.

"Clint, I want you to allow me to announce that I am godfather of Nito and Nicole. Please! And I would be greatly honored if you would be the godfather of my children."

"We don't have godfathers on the comarca."

"And?"

"And I am and would be honored."

They chatted awhile. Nito came in. Clint said that Qanar was his godfather. He thought about it and said, "We are more close than that."

The phone was on speaker. Qanar said that was the most moving thing that had ever been said to him. There was a catch in his voice.

Life was beautiful, if you let it be.

C. D. Moulton's works are available on most major outlets as printed or ebooks. CD writes the CD Grimes, PI, mysteries, the Det. Lt. Nick Storie mysteries, the Clint Faraday mysteries, the Flight of the Maita science fiction series, books on orchid culture and many others of many types. Mystery, adventure, intrigue, science fiction, humor, fantasy, paranormal, mild erotica, and factual.